THIS BOOK BELONGS TO

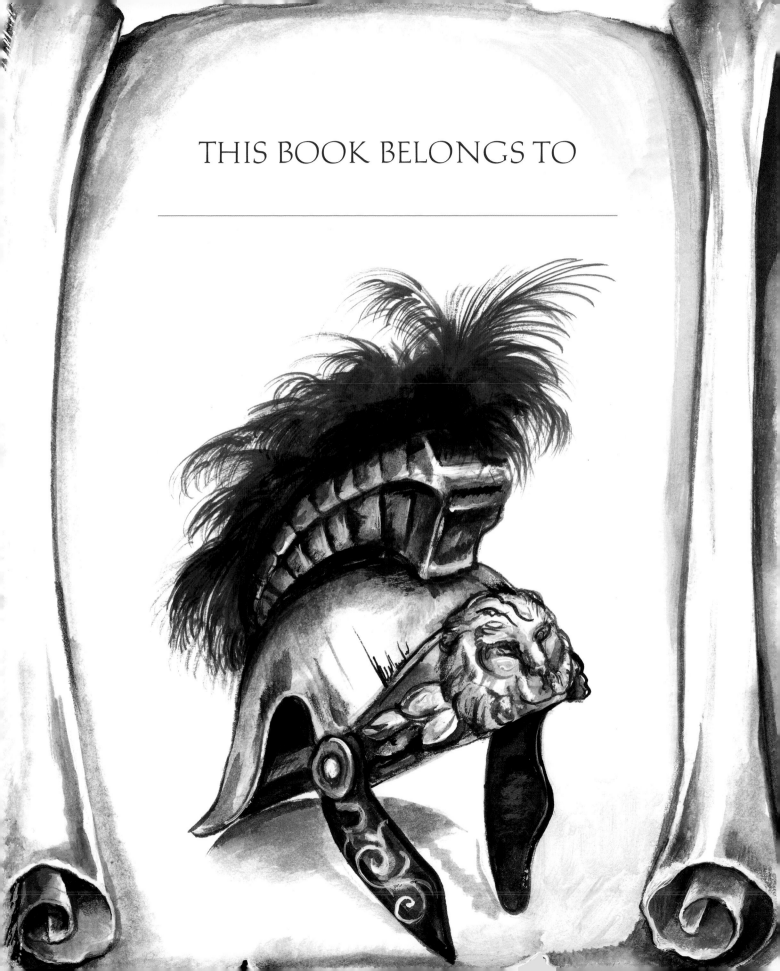

WOODSON

The Adventures of

Bella & Harry

Let's Visit Rome!

Written By

Lisa Manzione

Illustrated By

Kristine Lucco

Bella & Harry, LLC

www.BellaAndHarry.com
email: BellaAndHarryGo@aol.com

"I am a gladiator!

I am a gladiator!"

5

"**Harry**, who are you talking to?"

"I am practicing, Bella. I am a 'Roman Gladiator'!"

"**Harry**, gladiators have not been around for thousands of years. A long time ago, gladiators were a part of competitions that were held in large areas, usually with a crowd watching the competition. Today Harry, gladiators can only be found posing for pictures outside the Roman Colosseum or in history books."

"**Where** is the Roman Colosseum, Bella?"

"The Roman Colosseum is in Rome, Italy. Remember, Harry,
we visited Venice, Italy with our family earlier this year.
Italy is in Europe. A lot of people think Italy looks like a boot!

Let's look at the map before we get started.
See Harry, Rome is here."

"Yes, Bella, I see Rome and I think
Italy still looks like a boot!"

"I agree Harry, but Italy is a very fancy boot!"

PORTUGAL   SPAIN

ROME

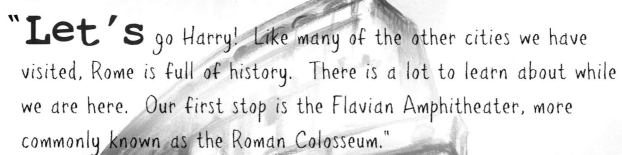

"**Let's** go Harry! Like many of the other cities we have visited, Rome is full of history. There is a lot to learn about while we are here. Our first stop is the Flavian Amphitheater, more commonly known as the Roman Colosseum."

"**Today**, the Colosseum is one of the most visited sites in Rome. The Colosseum is in ruins now, mostly because of earthquakes and stone robbers. There is not much left of the original floor, but you can still see the 'hypogeum' from the inside of the Colosseum."

"**Bella**, what is a 'hypogeum'?"

"A 'hypogeum' is an area underground. If you were a gladiator Harry, this is where you would have entered the stadium for your contest."

"**Most** people believe the Colosseum is one of the best buildings ever built by the Romans. The building is about 2,000 years old. It's an 'amphitheater', which means the building is usually oval or round, and there is no roof covering the center area of the theater."

"**Look** up there! That area is called Palatine Hill. Palatine Hill is one of the oldest areas in Rome. It is also one of the seven hills that Rome was built on. If you look below the hill, you will see the Roman Forum."

"We are going to the Roman Forum next. Come on, let's go!"

15

"**First**, the Roman Forum was a marketplace. Later Harry, many other buildings were built in and around the Roman Forum area during ancient times."

"**There** were all sorts of meetings held at the Roman Forum for both work and fun. Today, the Roman Forum is only ruins, but it too is one of the oldest areas of Rome."

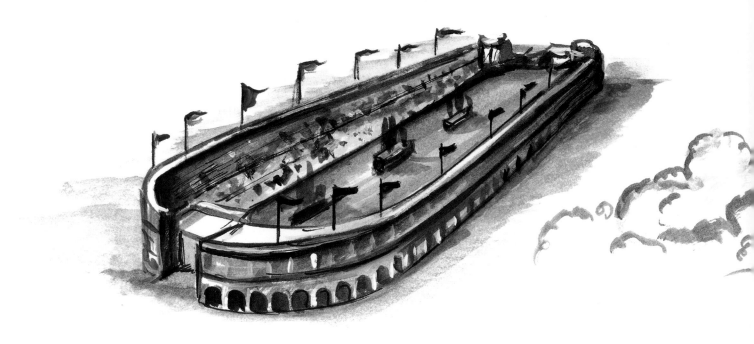

"**Next** stop, Circus Maximus!"

"Yay! I love the circus!"

18

"Harry, Circus Maximus is not a circus with animals or games. Circus Maximus was a place for chariot races long ago. It was the first and largest stadium in old Rome. It measures about 2,050 feet long ... or about 342 average lions ... standing tail to tail. It's now a public park."

"**Lunch** time! We are going to have lunch at Piazza Navona today. The piazza, or open square, has a big fountain, which has one obelisk (a four sided, tall stone) in the middle of the fountain."

"**There** are two more fountains at each end of the piazza. Also, there are a lot of places in the piazza that serve lunch and dinner."

"**It** looks like the antipasto (or first course) includes cheeses, meats, and olives... you know, all of your favorites!"

"Yummy!"

"**Let's** go Harry! It's time to see a famous fountain and toss a coin in the water!"

24

"**Harry**, this is the Trevi Fountain, or Fontana di Trevi. It is the largest and most famous Baroque (a type of design) fountain in Rome. I am going to turn around and toss this coin in the water.

Harry? Harry?"

25

"**Harry**, what are you doing? Get out of the water!"

"**Bella**, look at all of the coins I found!"

"Harry, no! People toss coins in the fountain because legend says if you toss a coin in the water, you will be sure to return to Rome. We must come back to Rome, so leave the coins in the water. There is so much more to see in this fun city! I am sure everyone who tossed a coin in the water wants to come back for another visit too!"

"Okay, Bella."

27

"**Harry**, we are now in an area called the 'Trident', which has lots of shopping and restaurants. Most of the streets in this area start with the name 'via', which means 'by way of' in our language."

WOODSON

29

"**Last** stop... the Spanish Steps! The Spanish Steps is a favorite location of both visitors and locals because of its beauty."

"The Spanish Steps make up the longest and widest staircase in Europe and they connect the lower piazza (Piazza di Spagna) with the upper piazza (Piazza Trinità dei Monti). Our hotel is located in the upper piazza, next to a beautiful old church. Let's race to the top!"

Whew! What a race! We are at our hotel at the top of the Spanish Steps. Harry and I are going to rest for a while after our fun tour of Rome. We can't wait for our next adventure but for now it's good-bye or "arrivederci" from Bella Boo and Harry too!

Our Adventure to Rome

Bella and Harry at the Pantheon.

Harry and Bella with the Vatican's Swiss Guard.

Bella and Harry enjoying spaghetti and meatballs.

Bella and Harry at the Vatican.

Fun Italian Words and Phrases

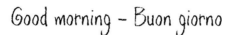

Yes – Si

No – No

Family – Famiglia

Good morning – Buon giorno

Good evening – Buona sera

Good night – Buona notte

Requests for permission to make copies of any part of the work should be directed to BellaAndHarryGo@aol.com or 855-235-5211.

Library of Congress Cataloging-in-Publications Data is available

Manzione, Lisa

The Adventures of Bella & Harry: Let's Visit Rome!

ISBN: 978-1-937616-08-3

First Edition

Book Eight of Bella & Harry Series

For further information please visit:

www.BellaAndHarry.com

or

Email: BellaAndHarryGo@aol.com

CPSIA Section 103 (a) Compliant

www.beaconstar.com/ consumer

ID: L0118329. Tracking No.: MR210171-1-10823

Printed in China